GIRLS SURVIVE

Girls Survive is published by Stone Arch Books, an imprint of Capstone.
1710 Roe Crest Drive
North Mankato, Minnesota 56003
www.capstonepub.com

Library of Congress Cataloging-in-Publication Data is available
on the Library of Congress website.

ISBN: 978-1-4965-8716-9 (hardcover)
ISBN: 978-1-4965-9217-0 (paperback)
ISBN: 978-1-4965-8717-6 (eBook PDF)

Summary:
Lily is a twelve-year-old Chinese American girl living in San Francisco's Chinatown when an earthquake destroys her home and sets her neighborhood on fire. Separated from her parents, Lily must help her younger brother escape San Francisco. As the city burns, Lily struggles to keep her group close as they face peril and racism. Will Lily make it across the bay to the safety of Oakland and be reunited with her parents?

Image Credits
Newscom: Rick E. Martin/TNS, 109; Shutterstock: Everett Historical, 105, 106, PATTERN PAPER PRINT, (pattern) design element throughout, Spalnic, (paper) design element throughout; Erin Summerill, 112

Designers: Cynthia Della-Rovere and Charmaine Whitman

LILY AND THE GREAT QUAKE

A San Francisco Earthquake Survival Story

by Veeda Bybee

illustrated by Alessia Trunfio

STONE ARCH BOOKS
a capstone imprint

CHAPTER ONE

Chinatown, San Francisco
April 17, 1906
Tuesday evening, 7:00 p.m.

I took a deep breath and *whoosh!* blew out tiny flames on a frosted pink cake. Out loud, I counted all twelve of the birthday candles in Mandarin, then in English.

Father clapped. "Your English sounds good! You are learning so much at school."

I ducked my chin and felt my cheeks warm. Everyone in the room was looking and smiling at me. Even though the attention was uncomfortable, it felt good to make Father proud.

"What else are you learning, Lily?" Mother asked. She bounced baby June on her hip.

All eyes were still on me. I know they wanted me to say something big and important, but I couldn't find the right words. I looked down at my hands and shrugged.

"Our shy Lily," Father said, his voice kind. "Just like the flower she was named after, she will choose her own time to bloom."

Hearing Father talking about me blossoming in front of everyone at my birthday celebration was so embarrassing. It made me want to shrivel up into a tiny ball. I didn't like when my parents talked about me like I wasn't there.

Just then, June fussed and screamed. The adults shifted their gazes toward her.

"There, there," Mother said, rocking June back and forth. My little sister was almost a year old. Mother said June's new teeth were coming in.

June's gums were sore, and it made her cranky. She also drooled a lot. Sometimes I wished I was like Baby June. Not afraid to fuss or scream or say how I felt. She was only a baby, but she was already braver than me.

Mother tore off a section of a soft bao bun and handed it to June. My little sister grabbed the white, fluffy dough and bit down. Little pieces of soggy bread clung to her chin.

Lee, my seven-year-old brother, laughed. "June is a flying mess!"

Mother frowned. "Your English is coming from those Penny Dreadful stories," she answered in Mandarin. "You sound like a western cowboy."

Lee's eyes lit up. "Yippee!" he whooped.

I covered my mouth to hide my laugh. Lee was wearing a straw cowboy hat. It was his most prized possession. He liked to ride around our home on a broom, pretending it was a horse. He wanted to have his own horse more than anything in the world. Father had to keep him from trying to pet the workhorses pulling wagons in the streets.

Mother shook her head and looked over at Father. "Where did you get this cake?"

Father smiled and touched June's chubby cheeks. Then he placed his big hands on my shoulders. "Mr. Mason gave it to me," he said. "He came into the store today. He knew it was Lily's birthday and wanted to contribute to the party."

Mr. Mason, a friend of Father's, would often ask about us. It was nice to know he cared. Not all people in San Francisco were kind to those who lived in Chinatown. Having this birthday treat from the Masons was special.

My family lived in a tiny apartment above our grocery store on Commercial Street. In our store, we sold all sorts of produce, like ginger, potatoes, and spices. It had been my grandparents' store, and now it belonged to my parents. Like Father, Mother was born in the United States. She helped Father run the family store. She was just as chatty as Father, and they had good relationships with many of their customers, including a few Americans.

Tonight, Father brought fresh fish from the market to share with our neighbors. Since our living space was larger than most, we could sometimes gather here for special occasions like my birthday.

I looked around the room while Mother took the cake away to cut. Our home was filled with neighbors from our building. Some attended the same Presbyterian church we went to. Others, like Mr. Quan who lived on the floor above us, had become good friends.

Mr. Quan was elderly. He had white streaks in his long black braid and wrinkles that looked like small smiles when he laughed. Mr. Quan's family was still in China. He had children and a wife back home and hadn't seen them in years, but he regularly sent them money. He liked to give Lee and me little candies. He said it was like he was giving sweets to his own son and daughter.

Father held out his hands. "Let's eat!"

The neighbors each brought food to share. Someone brought large bowls filled with rice. Another person contributed noodles with bits of pork. Our apartment smelled of fried garlic and savory vegetables. I couldn't eat fast enough with my chopsticks. I wanted to taste every dish.

When we finished our dinner, Mother passed out tiny pieces of cake to everyone in the room. The cake was bright yellow with pink icing.

I took a bite of cake and closed my eyes. The frosting was smooth and creamy. The cake had a bright flavor, bursting of lemon. It was an explosion of sweet and tangy. I had never tasted anything so wonderful.

After everyone had their last bite, Mr. Quan held out a present. "This is from all of us in the building."

I traced my fingers over the newspaper. There was an ink drawing of horses running all along the newsprint. Mr. Quan loved art. He would sit outside the building and draw on whatever paper he could find. I stared at his horses. Their manes blew around them, and some stood on hind legs. They looked so wild and free.

"It's so beautiful," I whispered, holding up the wrapped present.

Mother nudged me gently. "Open it, Lily."

I carefully peeled off the wrapping. The paper was stuck together with a bit of mashed rice. I wanted to keep this drawing of the horses forever. I already knew where it would hang—in the front room, right above the seating area where Lee and I slept.

He could pretend to be a cowboy riding wild horses, and I could imagine being free like the horses, who could roam anywhere they wanted. One day, I wanted to go further than the restrictions of Chinatown. Who knows? Maybe I would go across the ocean.

Father laughed. "Lily is so happy to have this drawing, and she hasn't seen the present yet!"

I felt another blush creeping up my face. I gently pulled off the paper.

I gasped. A hardbound book. *"The Wonderful Wizard of Oz!"*

I wrapped my arms around the book and hugged it hard. The neighbors all laughed, but I didn't care this time.

At school, we had read this story about a little girl named Dorothy who was swept away by a cyclone in Kansas and transported to a far-off land. I had never owned a hardback copy of a book before. They were expensive, and my family was very poor.

I flipped through the pages of the book. The illustrations were so magical, and it was all mine to study! I didn't have to worry about giving it up for another student to borrow. This was a book just for me.

I loved the story about the Land of Oz. I liked how Dorothy was brave. She had gone on a journey to find her way home, following a yellow brick road in search of a wizard. Along the way, she made new friends and defeated the Wicked Witch of the West. I wished I could be like her.

"Thank you all so very much." I bowed my head to my neighbors.

They all smiled. I would treasure this book forever.

After we helped clear the dishes, Lee and I snuggled next to each other on the floor. It was late, and candles were lit. The adults lowered their voices.

Their murmurs sounded like a steady stream of water flowing all around me. I loved hearing them talk in Mandarin about their lives back home in China. When Lee and I were home, we spoke Mandarin like everyone else. But when it was just the two of us, we tried to speak English. Lee wanted to sound like a cowboy, and I wanted to practice.

"The Americans are doing everything they can to displace us," Mr. Quan said. "Remember the bubonic plague? Just two years ago they were roping off Chinatown and blaming us for the disease."

"We fought the barriers in court and won," Father said. "They had to take those ropes down."

"It's not stopping them from spreading more rumors," Mr. Quan said. "I heard city officials are trying to kick us out. Move us to another part of town—to the outskirts of the city."

I turned my head so I could watch the adults. I didn't understand why the Americans hated us so much.

"Mr. Mason says some people are afraid to come to Chinatown," Father said. "There are those who say it is dirty and uncivilized. They call us vermin, wild animals who carry disease. They say there are too many Chinese crammed in this neighborhood."

In 1882, a law called the Chinese Exclusion Act was passed, and it prevented Chinese people from moving to the United States. We were one of the few Chinese families in San Francisco with children. Like Mr. Quan, we had family back in China. I had never met Mother's older sisters and brothers. They had returned to China and, because of the Chinese Exclusion Act, could not come back. We didn't know if we would ever see them again.

Mother clucked her tongue. She rocked June to sleep. "Where else are we supposed to live?" she said. "Of course we are crowded. The laws prevent us from moving anywhere else in the city. Anyway, I bet Chinatown is just as clean as the other parts of San Francisco."

For decades, Chinese immigrants had been coming to America to find better jobs. They worked on the railroads, mined for gold, or did housekeeping. The American dollar was worth a lot. People from all over the world were moving to the United States for new opportunities. Now, because of the law, Chinese people were the only ones who were not legally allowed to move to the United States.

Next to me, Lee stirred. "My stomach hurts," he whispered. "I think I ate too much."

I opened up my new book. I could see the words from the glow of the candlelight.

"How about I read to you?" I asked.

Lee rested his head on my shoulder. "Spin me a yarn, little lady." He looked up at me. "That means tell a story."

I giggled. Lee could always make me smile, even when things felt sad. "All right, cowboy."

I opened up to the first page. There was an illustration of a young girl with braided pigtails, looking out over a vast field.

"Dorothy lived in the midst of the great Kansas prairies," I read in English. "With Uncle Henry, who was a farmer, and Aunt Em, who was the farmer's wife."

The room was quiet. The adults had stopped talking and turned their heads in my direction. Seeing them watch, I froze and stopped reading. I wanted to hide.

"Keep going," Mother said. "You're a great storyteller."

They weren't my own words, I reminded myself, but the author's. I could read out loud and practice my English. I hesitated, then took a deep breath.

"Okay," I said.

My words came out slow at first, but soon I forgot people were listening. I got lost in the story of Dorothy's ordinary life in Kansas with her family and dog, Toto. Before I knew it, I had read a few pages. I stopped reading right when the cyclone came down from the sky.

Lee was asleep next to me.

I looked at my parents. "Do you think we will ever get a cyclone here, like the one in my book?"

"In San Francisco," Father said, "our greatest threat is earthquakes."

Mr. Quan slapped his knees. "We've crossed

an ocean to get here and survived mine explosions. A little earth shaking can't drive us away!"

Mr. Quan was like Lee. He made everyone smile.

I knew that minor tremors were common in California. They were so frequent that sometimes Lee and I joked that it felt like a cable car was running loose past our apartment. With all the noise from our get-together tonight, I wondered if I had missed a small earthquake already.

It was time for our neighbors to leave. My parents said goodbye to everyone, and I pulled the blankets over me, ready to go to sleep. Suddenly I heard a terrible screeching sound. It sounded like an animal yowling, scared or in pain.

CHAPTER **TWO**

Chinatown, San Francisco
April 17, 1906
Tuesday night, 9:00 p.m.

Lee woke up immediately. He blinked away
his sleep and crawled to the window. "It's cats!"
he said. "They are going crazy out there, like
wild horses!"

He opened the window, and the howling grew
louder. I covered my ears as I hurried over to the
window. He was right. This horrible noise was
coming from the alley cats. They were acting so
strange!

The cats ran around in circles, like they didn't know where they wanted to escape to. They screamed and howled as though their tails were on fire.

The eerie sound sent a chill through me.

"They sound like something is attacking them!" I said.

Lee scrunched up his face and yowled. "Rrawwwwwwwwww!"

I laughed, even though it felt more scary than funny.

"Lee!" Mother said. "Lily! Leave those poor cats alone and go to sleep."

I shut the window. Lee and I scooted close to each other.

I was so tired from the party, my eyes felt heavy with exhaustion. I went to sleep, dreaming of cats and cyclones and cake.

Outside, the cats still howled.

A witch in black clothes rushed toward me. She screamed, and I couldn't move. I watched her hurl forward in the sky, waving her hands round and round, creating a cyclone.

The winds whirled in our living room. I held my hands up to keep plates from smashing into me. The sound of broken glass crashed around my ears, along with the piercing whistle of an oncoming train.

"Lily, Lily!"

I opened my eyes. Lee was shaking me. He dug his fingers into my arm, pinching me.

"Ouch," I yelled. "You're hurting me!"

Lee was breathing fast. His eyes were wide. He looked terrified.

I sat up. There was still roaring in my ears.

The room continued to shake. Was I still dreaming? Was the Wicked Witch real? Was there really a cyclone in my house? I grabbed Lee's arm and patted his face. He didn't feel like a dream.

"Lee," I said, holding on to my brother, "what's going on?"

Right as Lee opened his mouth, a large chunk of our ceiling crashed down.

We both screamed. Lee threw his arms around me and held on tight. We tried to get to our feet, but quickly fell down. Smaller pieces of plaster were coming down fast, pelting us like hail.

The building groaned and shook beneath me. The rumbling was loud and thunderous and seemed to come from everywhere. It was more terrible than a witch's scream.

There was a loud cracking sound, and a wood beam split from our ceiling. One part still held on. Another piece swung into the kitchen, bashing into a counter. A plate I had washed the night before tumbled to the ground. Then another plate and another. Dishes shattered all over the floor.

Pictures came off the wall. Furniture tipped over. Our home seemed to be coming apart.

"We need to get to Mother and Father!" I said to Lee. But every time we tried to stand, we were knocked to our knees.

I looked down the hall, in the direction of our parents' room. I thought I heard them call to me. When I tried to yell to them, the noise was so loud I couldn't hear my own voice. I wasn't sure if I was even talking.

The room swayed, rolling like waves in the ocean. My stomach lurched. I knew we needed to get to safety. I grabbed Lee by the arm. "Under the table!"

I wasn't sure if Lee could hear me, but he followed my lead. On our hands and knees, I pushed past broken plates and crawled toward the kitchen table.

Where are my parents? I thought. *What about June? She wouldn't be able to help herself to safety.*

Just in time, Lee and I scrambled under the table. Right then, the remaining wood beam fell from the ceiling. It crashed down on the blanket I had been under just moments ago.

From under the table, I saw my copy of *The Wonderful Wizard of Oz.* I watched it slide across the floor in my direction.

Letting go of Lee's hand, I quickly crawled out into the open and grabbed it. Then I scrambled back under the table with Lee, my book clutched tightly in one arm.

Suddenly, there was a loud *thud.* Something heavy had fallen onto the table above us. One of the table legs splintered from the weight. Lee and I screamed even though we knew no one could hear us.

CHAPTER **THREE**

Chinatown, San Francisco
April 18, 1906
Wednesday morning, 5:14 a.m.

Dust filled my lungs. I coughed. "Lee!" I shouted.

I stretched my arms out until I felt the rough cotton sleeve of my brother's shirt. I pulled him in close. "Are you all right?" I asked.

Lee groaned. "I think so. I can't see anything."

The room was no longer shaking, but Lee was. We were buried underneath our kitchen table. But we were alive.

"What happened?" Lee said.

"I think we were in an earthquake," I said. "This table saved us."

"Lily, where are Mother and Father?" he asked.

I pressed against the chunks of plaster and fallen bricks that surrounded the kitchen table. "Somewhere on the other side," I said.

All around us was rubble. We had no idea what the rest of our house looked like.

"We are trapped," Lee said. I heard a quiver in his voice.

I ran my hands along the wall of debris. "It feels like chunks of the wall and ceiling," I said.

"Are we going to get out?" he asked.

I couldn't find any words to answer Lee. They seemed stuck in my throat. Even at really important times like this one, I couldn't find the right things to say.

"Lily! Lee!" Somewhere in the room, Father was calling for us. He sounded far away.

"Under here!" Lee shouted. "Under the table!"

I pounded on the underside of the table. Lee did too. I heard my father grunt. He was right next to us, but hidden behind the rubble.

The room shook again. I braced myself, placing my palms on the floor.

"Is this another earthquake?" Lee asked.

"Don't worry," Father said, his voice was muffled. "I'll get you out."

I heard the hard pattering of many tiny pieces of debris hitting the top of the kitchen table.

Lee grabbed my arm. "What was that?"

I didn't know how to answer him. I wanted to be brave, but I was scared too.

After a few seconds, the shaking stopped.

"Are you both okay?" Father said.

"Yes," Lee said.

From the other side of the rubble, different voices joined Father. I heard Mr. Quan's familiar grumble. It was our neighbors. They groaned as they tried to move the heavy debris around us.

I heard a familiar cry. It was fussy and angry. Baby June!

Even though my sister was cranky, it was a relief to hear her voice. I strained to hear one more.

"Father!" I shouted. "Where is Mother?"

Father couldn't hear me. He was talking to the neighbors. Their voices were further away and muffled.

Lee started to sniffle.

I reached out to feel his face. "Father is right there, and he will get us out."

"This is so scary," he said.

In the dark, I felt around the floor until I found my book. Even though I couldn't see the pages, I remembered the story. "Do you remember the Cowardly Lion in *The Wonderful Wizard of Oz*?" I asked.

"Yeah," Lee said. "He was a big 'fraidy cat, right?"

"It's okay to be afraid," I said. "We can face our fears just like that lion."

I pressed against the wall of debris. "Let's get out of here."

Lee and I did our best to help. We worked hard, clawing our way through broken pieces of plaster. My hands and arms felt sore. It felt like we had been trapped for days.

Soon, little cracks in the rubble turned into bigger slices of light.

I could see Father. He was moving fast, clearing away debris to get to us. "Almost there!" he said. "Just a little more."

I took my book and pounded at the wall. I used the hardback cover to clear away more rocks. The openings grew bigger. I could finally see Father's face.

"Are you both okay?" Father asked. He was caked with dust and dried blood.

"Yes," I said.

"We will get you out, Lily," Father said.

Another tremor rocked the room. They were coming close together now. We needed to get out of the building.

"How long have we been stuck here?" I asked.

Father's eyes found mine. "We've been trying to get you out for quite a while. And we will."

I believed him. I picked up my book and started pounding again. Soon, there was a hole big enough to push my hand through. I felt the warm grip of my father's hand. Then there was another hole through the debris and another hand.

I continued to use my book to chip away at the debris. As I imagined the plaster tearing at the edges of my hardback book, I winced. Better my book than my hands, though.

Lee was using debris to scrape away at the wall.

"That's a good idea," I said and put my book down.

As we worked, bits of wall came off into our hands. Some plaster pieces crumbled into our space beneath the table.

The opening was finally big enough to wiggle through. I was free!

As soon as I got out, Father reached for Lee.

When Lee was safe, I threw my arms around Father. He nestled his face into my hair.

"Going under the table was very smart. You are so brave," he said.

I took a deep breath, exhausted. We must have been trapped for hours. Broken items littered the floor.

Just then, the building shook. It was stronger this time. Father grabbed Lee and me. More pieces of plaster fell around us.

Father handed me a laundry basket. "I collected some extra clothes and food for you and Lee. I already have some things for Mother and June and myself."

I looked at Father. "Where are Mother and June?"

"They are waiting outside," Father said.

Mr. Quan came to what was left of the apartment door. "We need to get out now," he said. "There are fires all around the city. You can see the smoke in the skies already."

I carefully walked through the debris to look out the window. I could see rooftops caved in. Two-story buildings were leveled to the ground. People were outside, making their way out of Chinatown. Mr. Quan was right. A thick cloud of smoke settled over the city.

"Have you seen my hat?" Lee said as he looked around frantically.

I glanced around the room. "No."

I saw Father tuck papers under his shirt. "What are those?" I asked.

"Legal documents," he said. "The last thing we need is for these to be destroyed. It's hard enough to be legal Chinese workers here. Imagine what they will do to us if we no longer have our paperwork."

I took my copy of *The Wonderful Wizard of Oz* and placed it in the laundry basket. I remembered my birthday party just hours before. It felt so long ago now.

"Oh no!" I said, glancing around the room. "The drawing of the horses is missing."

"I still can't find my cowboy hat!" Lee said.

Another tremor rocked the building.

"Forget the drawing and the hat," Father ordered. "We need to get out *now*!"

CHAPTER FOUR

Chinatown, San Francisco
April 18, 1906
Wednesday, 12:00 p.m.

I barreled outside, eager to see my mother. When I got to the street, I spotted her resting on a pile of crates. Mother looked pale. Her eyes were closed.

"Mother!" I wrapped my arms around her but quickly let go when she flinched. "What happened?"

"One of my legs is hurt," she said. "I can't walk on it." Mother held my arm. "Don't worry, I have plenty of help. And June has been great company."

I looked down at my baby sister asleep in Mother's arms. I shook my head. I had no idea how she could sleep through the commotion in the streets. June didn't care what anyone thought. She would take a nap whenever she wanted.

I sat down on the crate next to Mother and took in Chinatown. It looked upside down. Buildings had collapsed into one another. Market stands had turned over. Fallen bricks and rocks were everywhere.

I thought about *The Wonderful Wizard of Oz*, and how after the cyclone, Dorothy saw two feet sticking out from under the bottom of a building. The feet belonged to the Wicked Witch of the East, who was crushed by a falling house. I didn't want to study these broken structures too closely. I didn't want to see anyone's limbs sticking out of the debris.

Father was talking with a neighbor. "Chinatown is nothing like some parts of San Francisco," the man said. "There are some areas where the homes are completely gone."

"This means we can come back," Father said. "After the fires are put out, we can come back and rebuild."

I looked at our building. The grocery store was still standing, and the apartment was still there. Somewhere in our home was Lee's hat and my horse drawing.

"I am going to the temple to pray," the man said to Father. "Come join us. Or are you going to your church?"

Father stood by Mother. "I need to find a ride out of Chinatown," he said. "You should leave too."

The man waved Father away. "It is not that bad," he said. "We will stay with our homes."

As he turned to leave, Mr. Quan came up to Father. Jade See Young, a young woman who lived in our building, handed Lee and me a bowl of rice with some meat and vegetables.

"Please eat," she said, her voice soft.

My stomach growled. I hadn't realized how hungry I was. It was already time for lunch. We had spent all morning trying to dig out from under the table.

With my fingers, I scooped bits of rice into my mouth. It was cold but very welcome. It almost tasted just as good as my birthday meal from last night.

"Thank you," I said to Jade. I felt shy talking to her.

Jade didn't come out often. She was not married. Jade was very traditional, and she had bound feet. This means her feet were wrapped tight with cloth and broken to keep from growing bigger. It was a custom that came from China. Some of the more traditional Chinese believed that women who had small feet were most beautiful. But having bound feet made it harder to walk.

Once, I was behind her going up our staircase.

It took her a very long time to shuffle up to her floor.

I tried to give some of my food to Mother.

Father stopped me. "I have food saved for her," he said. "You take that for yourself."

He knelt down, so he was the same height as Lee and me. "I've talked with our neighbors. We all agree we need to leave Chinatown. Mr. Quan heard that the fires are spreading quickly through the city. We also have to watch out for the aftershocks."

"Aftershocks?" Lee said.

"Yes," Father said. "Aftershocks are smaller earthquakes that happen after a big one. They can be just as dangerous."

I swallowed and looked up at our apartment window. An aftershock could do more damage. Or our house might burn. I might no longer have a home.

"Where are we going to go?" Lee said.

"Oakland," Father said. "My cousin works on a fishing boat across the bay. We can stay with him."

I watched Mother, who still had her eyes closed. I was worried we might lose our home, but I was even more worried and scared to see Mother suffering.

"How will Mother get there?" I said.

"Mr. Quan is trying to get in touch with his friend who has a cart," he said. "We are going to wheel her to safety."

He placed a hand on my shoulder. "Lily, we decided the best thing to do is to divide up. We will make our way to the waterfront and meet again at the Ferry Building. You and Lee will go with Mr. Quan and Jade See Young. I've given them some provisions from the store to take care of you and Lee."

"No!" Lee yelled and clung to Father's arm. "I don't want to leave you."

Father hugged him. "I don't either, but your mother cannot walk. She needs a ride. But it really isn't safe to stay if you are able to leave."

How could my strong mother suddenly be so helpless? How could Chinatown look so different from one day to the next? I knew I needed to be confident for Lee, but I didn't know how. I wanted to cling to Father and cry too. Instead, I took a deep breath.

"We'll meet in front of the Ferry Building. We can find transportation from there to Oakland," Father said. He put his arm around Lee and me. "We will all get on a boat together."

He looked down the road, past St. Mary's Church. I followed my father's gaze. The church was still standing, but the cross was no longer on top of the steeple. I could see flickering flames in the distance. They seemed to dance on the rooftops but looked too far away to cause any harm.

"The firemen can put the fire out, right?" I asked.

Father looked worried. "I hope so. I worry about the fires coming so close to our home."

Lee wouldn't let go of Father.

"We will meet you at the Ferry Building," I said. "Come on, Lee. We will be okay."

Father nodded. "Come say goodbye to Mother," he said.

Lee and I approached Mother. When I held her hand, she opened her eyes. They were deep brown, just like mine.

"Here are my brave ones," Mother said. Her voice was tired. "I am proud of you both. Let me give you both something." She leaned forward and gave us each a kiss on our foreheads. "For protection."

I looked up. My mother remembered the beginning of my favorite story.

"Like in *The Wonderful Wizard of Oz*," I said. "The good witch gives Dorothy a kiss for safety."

"Yes." Mother smiled. "No one will injure a person kissed by the Good Witch of the North. I think it goes something like that."

I touched the place where Mother had kissed me.

"Instead of following a brick road," Mother said. "You will follow the San Francisco streets to the Ferry Building."

Father and the neighbors were starting to form their groups.

Mr. Quan waved to us. "Time to go!" he shouted.

Resting the basket against my hip, I took Lee's hand in mine.

He looked up at me. "Are you ready, little lady?"

"You betcha, cowboy." I heard my voice shake. We were both pretending.

With that, we left our parents and headed toward the waterfront. I hoped we would see them again.

CHAPTER FIVE

San Francisco
April 18, 1906
Wednesday, 1:00 p.m.

The streets were crowded.

As I walked through the city, the devastation
was surprising. There was even more damage here
than in Chinatown. Homes sunk into the earth.
Buildings tilted at strange angles. It seemed like just
one breeze might topple them over.

I was shocked to see some walls completely
gone, leaving interior rooms exposed. I could see
straight into bedrooms. Living rooms. Kitchens.
It reminded me of looking into a dollhouse, except
the people inside were real.

Everyone was frantic. They called out for loved ones. Some were crying. Others shouted that the world was ending. Some dragged various belongings behind them. Someone pushed a toy wagon full of plants down the street. Another person dragged a trunk behind them.

There were many injured. Some were helping those who were down. Others laid still in the street. Some were still trapped. Just like the Wicked Witch of the East, they were buried under what was left of their homes. I looked away when I saw a wagon that was tipped over. A horse lay on its side, with bricks piled on top.

When Lee saw the dead horse, he cried.

As we walked, masses of people crowded the street, all heading in the same direction we were. "Hold on to my shirt," I told Lee. "Don't let go."

I worried that the force of the crowd would separate us. It was already creating distance between us and Mr. Quan. Jade See Young stayed near the two of us.

I saw Mr. Quan turn his head back in search of us. Every now and then, we would make eye contact. I knew he was trying to keep us in his sight.

It was difficult to keep up with him. His long braid kept getting further away. Many people in the streets were much taller than me. Jade walked slowly near Lee and me. She had on traditional Chinese clothing with a beautiful silver comb tucked into her hair. I noticed Jade was having a hard time keeping up. She wore wooden shoes and hobbled with each step.

My mother had warned me not to look down on others for differences that seemed strange to me. "Women of all cultures have been doing things throughout history to make themselves more attractive," Mother had said. "However, this is something your father and I do not want to pass on to our children."

The crowds grew bigger until I could no longer see Mr. Quan. Jade was no longer nearby. I could barely see in front of me.

Lee tugged on my sleeve. "Lily," Lee said. "Where is Mr. Quan?"

I swallowed. Following the yellow brick road was hard when I could barely see the streets. I didn't want my brother to hear the panic rising up in my chest. I tried to keep my voice calm.

"Just ahead of us," I said. "Let's walk on the outside of this group so we can see better."

I tried to scoot closer to the edge of the crowd, but I couldn't move more than a couple steps.

A woman pushed in front of me. She wore many layers of clothing and dragged a tied up bundle behind her, filled with whatever valuables she wanted to save. I almost tripped on it.

"Out of my way!" the woman shouted.

I clutched my laundry basket tighter. I saw the cover of my book, with the Tin Woodman holding an ax. In the story, the Tin Woodman didn't think he was very useful. With his ax, he chopped down trees and enemies. He ended up using his ax to help Dorothy along her journey through the Land of Oz.

I had an idea. I held my laundry basket close to my chest. Like the Tin Woodman, it would be my ax. I would chop through this crowd.

I turned to Lee. "Whatever you do," I said, "don't let go of my shirt."

Using the basket to help, I pushed my way past a man wearing a black top hat. He looked surprised to see me.

I wrinkled my brow in concentration and ordered, "Out of my way!" Remarkably, the crowd let us through.

Shouting like this filled me with confidence. I could hardly speak up in school or at home, yet here I was yelling at strangers. The most amazing thing was that they were listening.

Maybe Father was right. I was beginning to bloom.

Soon, Lee and I were at the edge of the crowd. I could see better from the outskirts. I climbed on top of a pile of wood to get a better idea of our surroundings.

It was a strange sight. People were dressed in all manner of clothing. Some wore pajamas. A man had on a full suit. People dragged trunks behind them. I watched a couple load up a baby crib full of belongings.

One family had piled their things on top of a piano and pushed it in front of them. People were using whatever they could find to save their things.

Lee climbed up beside me. "Whoa, there," he said with a western drawl. "This place looks like a train wreck."

"You got that right, cowboy," I said.

The city looked wrong. Things were everywhere, as if houses had just been picked up, shaken, and their contents dropped onto the streets. There was a broken plate in the road. A singular shoe by a

window. An expensive-looking doll with silky
yellow hair laid on the street. Her blue eyes were
wide open and part of her porcelain face was
smashed to pieces.

Cable cars were turned on their sides, and their
twisted tracks snaked around the streets.

Not being so close to others, I thought the
air would smell better. In the center of the street,

I had only smelled the sweat of the people around me. Now, I could smell the smoke. I realized the air was thick with it. "Where are the fires?" I asked Lee.

A man wearing a fancy vest pulled a wagon packed with household items. He looked up at me on the wood pile. "All over the city," he said. "The firemen have no water to stop it. All the lines are down."

I nodded. I was surprised he was talking to me. The man seemed surprised to be talking to me too.

"Are you coming from Chinatown?" the man asked. "Your English is real good. I have never seen so many Chinese girls. There was one right behind us."

Most white people in San Francisco rarely went to Chinatown, so they didn't often see Chinese people.

Maybe it was that he had complimented my

English, or maybe it was because of everything I had been through already this morning, but I didn't feel embarrassed to talk to this man. "Yes," I said. "We are joining our family at the Ferry Building."

"Our parents are waiting for us," Lee said.

The man nodded. "Good luck to the both of you."

I started to walk away, then quickly turned around. "Wait! Did you say you saw another Chinese girl?"

I couldn't believe how bold I was, making conversation with an adult.

"Yes," the man said. "She's walking really slow. Just a little further back."

I knew that he was talking about Jade. She must have fallen even farther behind. We had been walking for hours now. Because of the size of the crowd, it was a slow journey.

"Watch out!" someone yelled as a bag came crashing down from the sky. When it hit the ground, tobacco pipes and books tumbled out. Lee and I jumped away just in time.

A woman poked her head out of a second-story window.

People shook their fists up at the houses. "You watch where you're throwing!"

"Folks chucking their belongings out their windows," the man in the fancy vest muttered. "Never thought I would see the day. Don't they realize there are people in the streets?"

He disappeared into the crowd.

"Jade is somewhere back there," I said to Lee.

"Lily!" Lee jumped up and down. "I think I see Mr. Quan! Let's find him first and come back for Jade."

Lee grabbed my shirt, and we both ran toward the front of the crowd. With my laundry basket,

I pushed my way through the mass of people and made a path to Mr. Quan.

But right as I was about to reach him, there were screams from behind us, followed by the sound of people running.

CHAPTER SIX

A large black steer came racing through the crowd. Its hooves pounded loudly on the streets and people were yelling, desperate to get out of way.

"Move!" someone shouted.

I grabbed my brother by the shoulder. "Hurry, Lee!" I yelled. "There's a wild steer!"

We quickly pushed our way to the side of the street, just in time for the animal to rush past. The long horns almost caught my shirt. The steer ran farther up the road. The crowd scattered everywhere, but I couldn't see what happened.

I held on to my brother. After the crowd had settled down, I looked around. I slowly realized that I didn't recognize a single person around us. Lee and I were separated from our group—again. And to make matters worse, now my basket was missing.

"Lee!" I said. "I dropped our basket somewhere!"

Lee straightened his shirt. He looked around and saw a cable car tipped over nearby, which he jumped on top of.

"I see it!" he said. "Follow me!" Then he took off running.

He must be imagining he's a hero in one of his stories, I thought as I followed him, pushing people aside. When I found Lee, he had already picked up the basket.

"You really are a cowboy," I said with a laugh. "You led us right to the basket, like you were roping in cattle."

Lee grinned. "Just you wait till I'm back on my horse again."

Right then, a couple people stopped in front of us.

"Did you hear?" a woman asked. "The fires are spreading! The firemen are blowing up Chinatown to contain it!"

"Why are they doing that?" another person said. "Not that I disagree with it. That place is filthy."

Lee and I stopped laughing and stood still.

"Good riddance to those vermin," a woman chimed in. "They have brought so much disease and crime to the city. I hope the fires clear them out."

Lee and I were standing close to them. Other Chinese people were walking in the crowd too. These people didn't care who heard them.

The man in the vest that I had talked to before

was suddenly next to me. "I'm sorry about your home," he said.

"Why are they doing this?" Lee said. "I thought firemen are supposed to help save homes, not blow them up."

The man shrugged. "The main water lines in the city are broken," he said. "We have no water. The firemen are making a firebreak to keep the fires from spreading. They think that by demolishing some buildings now, it will save others."

I looked back in direction of Chinatown. "I wish it didn't have to be our homes that were sacrificed."

There were multiple fires raging in the city. The air was thick with smoke. I could feel the heat from the fires even though they were far away. At least, I hoped they were.

As I watched the smoke swirl in the distant sky,

I thought it likely that my family would never share a meal at our kitchen table again.

I didn't get a chance to say goodbye to the apartment or our grocery store. We didn't have much, but it was still our home. I couldn't imagine it gone.

Lee and I held on to the laundry basket as we continued to walk. We had been walking all day. My legs were sore. My arms hurt from carrying the basket.

With news of the destruction of Chinatown, Mother and Father felt even further away than before.

Lee turned to me. "Mother could still be home," he said. "Maybe we should go back and help her. It's what a proper cowboy would do."

An American woman in the crowd looked down at us. "Didn't you hear what they just said?" the woman said. "Chinatown will be gone soon! The National Guard has been sent there. They are making sure the area is free of looters. No one is entering Chinatown now. If they do, they will be killed." The woman wrinkled her face at Lee. "Not that there is anything to steal there anyway."

I pulled Lee away from the woman. It was my responsibility to protect my brother, and these people didn't feel safe.

"Don't listen to them," I said.

"So, can we go back?" Lee asked.

I frowned. "No. We need to stick to the plan. Besides, if Mother and Father got a ride, they could be at the Ferry Building before us."

We kept on walking. No matter how many buildings I saw split open or how many streets I saw buckled up like hills, I couldn't get used to the destruction.

I hated every toppled brick. I knew it used to

belong to someone's house. I looked away from every stray shoe. I didn't want to think about what might have happened to the person who was missing it.

I tried to close my ears from every sad sob. It was hard to imagine who or what they were crying over. If I thought about these things, I would worry about everything I might've lost too—Mother, Father, June, our home. . . . I couldn't bear to think about how Chinatown would be no more. Or what would happen if we never saw our parents again.

I heard people talking loudly up ahead. There was a group of people bargaining with a man on a horse, pulling a wagon.

"How much for a ride to the ferry?" someone asked.

"One hundred dollars," the man on the horse replied.

"What!" Another man threw down his hat. "That is outrageous!"

They continued arguing until, eventually, the driver got his asking price—one hundred dollars. This worried me. How was Father going to get Mother to the Ferry Building? I knew my family did not have that kind of money.

Up ahead, I caught a glimpse of a woman shuffling along the street. A glint from a silver comb shone through the crowd. Jade! She must have moved ahead of us when the steer separated everyone in the crowd.

I pointed Jade out to Lee. He smiled for the first time in hours. Seeing Jade was a breath of fresh air, which we desperately needed on this smoke-filled day. Maybe Mr. Quan would be close too.

"Jade!" I called out. Lee and I rushed over. It didn't take us long to catch up.

Jade stopped when she heard her name. With all our shouting, we caught the attention of a few people nearby. As Lee and I ran up to her, a handful of Americans gathered around our friend.

One woman who was standing close to Jade said, "She's disgusting. Look at those horrible feet! I should kick her over."

The others around her laughed. I felt sick. These people reminded me of the winged monkeys in *The Wonderful Wizard of Oz*. The monkeys snatched up Dorothy and flew away with her. Here, this group flapped around poor Jade. They acted like Jade couldn't understand them, or maybe they didn't care if she did.

"Why don't you go back to China with the rats you brought over?" a young man snarled. He was close to Jade's face, practically spitting on her. "We don't want your kind here!"

I felt scared. I thought of the Scarecrow in *The Wonderful Wizard of Oz*. The Scarecrow felt like he didn't have a brain, and at this moment, I didn't know how to use mine. I was only twelve years old. I was a Chinese girl in a city full of people who hated me. How was I supposed to think of a plan to help Jade when I could barely help myself?

"Lily, we need to do something," Lee said, staring down the people who were harassing Jade. He looked angry.

He was right. No one should be treated this way. Practically everyone in the city had just lost their home. These people didn't need to spread hate around.

Even if I couldn't think of a plan, I knew I needed to speak up just like I had before. Following the streets of San Francisco was like Dorothy following the yellow brick road. It was making me a little braver.

With my basket, I pushed my way closer to Jade and the group of hecklers.

I stood tall and threw my basket to the ground. "Leave her alone!" I shouted in English.

CHAPTER SEVEN

San Francisco
April 18, 1906
Wednesday afternoon, 4:00 p.m.

The men and women surrounding Jade turned

their attention toward me. They looked startled.

"The city is burning, and you are picking on a

single woman, by herself!" I put my hands on my

hips.

I thought of the bossy woman who first pushed

me on the street. "Get out of my way!" I yelled.

The woman who had been snickering at Jade

minutes before stood there with her mouth open.

The others in the group also looked like they were

out of words.

I wondered what surprised them more, that my English was clear and loud, or that a twelve-year-old girl was standing up to their bullying.

My voice caused others in the crowd to look our way. People started to notice the group of people surrounding Jade. Men crossed their arms, and mothers held their children closer.

The bullies could see that others were not happy with them. They grumbled and dispersed.

As soon as they left, I took Jade by the hand. "Let's go," I said, and the three of us walked down the street together.

I kept my head held high. I had used my brains, just like the Scarecrow. I didn't have a plan, but I followed my heart like the Tin Woodman. I had courage like the Cowardly Lion and spoke up.

It was risky and scary, but I had used my words to fight my way.

With the mean people gone, we continued our

walk to the Ferry Building. Jade's bound feet had us traveling at a slow pace. I didn't mind. The basket was feeling heavier with every step. My legs felt like they couldn't carry me much longer.

The smoke from the fires made the San Francisco sky even grayer than usual. I didn't know if we would beat the fires. They seemed to creep closer and closer every time I looked behind me. I wondered if we would ever make it out of the city.

I listened to more conversations. I wasn't the only one who was worried about getting out of the fire's path.

It seemed like hours passed before I finally spotted the black, choppy waters of the San Francisco Bay. The area surrounding the Ferry Building was crowded. There were people everywhere, shouting and crying. Some were trying to sell things. Others were guarding their possessions.

Where was Mr. Quan? We were supposed to meet my family at the Ferry Building. How would we find anyone in this huge crowd?

Lee, Jade, and I found a small spot to rest. "I am so glad I can put this basket down," I said. "It's gotten so heavy."

Just then, someone bumped into Jade. Teetering on her wooden shoes, she lost her balance.

"Ahh!" Jade cried as she stepped into the middle of our laundry basket. The book, extra clothes, and food scattered across the grass. Before we could pick any of it up, someone walked over our food.

The man said something and disappeared into the mass of people around us. I couldn't tell if he was apologizing or making a snide remark.

Someone else snickered. "Go home," she muttered.

I picked up the scattered clothing, whatever food

I could salvage, and my book, and placed them in the basket.

"Come on," I said to Jade and Lee. "Let's go find somewhere else to rest. I don't think we should be close to these people while we are sleeping."

Over the next few hours, we wandered around the Ferry Building in search of my parents, Mr. Quan, or anyone else we knew. We also tried to find a good place to rest. As the sky grew dark, we finally found a patch of grass just big enough for the three of us to lie down. Sitting on the ground, we finished off the remainder of our food.

I took my last bite of rice and turned to Lee and Jade. "Stay here," I said. "I'm going to walk around one more time. It will be easier to go alone. I can cover more ground."

"Come back, Lily," Lee begged.

"Of course I will," I said. "Maybe I'll even bring back some good news."

In the twilight, the crowd of people seemed bigger. Their voices were louder, and the cries from those who were suffering grew even more piercing.

I realized it might be hard to find Lee and Jade in the dark. I didn't go far. The last thing I wanted was to lose them again.

I walked by many people and caught strains of conversations in English and Chinese.

"My entire building crumbled," a Chinese man said. "I don't think the people on the bottom floor survived."

"I heard anyone returning to Chinatown was shot," another Chinese man said. "They were being chased out, accused of being looters."

I went a little farther around the building. Still no sight of my parents. I overheard a white man with whiskers talking to another white man. "My dog ran into our house to save us." He wiped away tears. "He never came back out."

"It's not the earthquake that is causing the most damage," a woman said. "But the fires that have started after."

"I heard the large fire in Hayes Valley was started by someone making breakfast," the woman's friend said. "She didn't know her chimney was broken. Her house caught fire, then the neighbors'. Just like that, the whole block was in flames. The earthquake broke water and gas lines. Now there is no water to put out the fires that are happening all over the city."

I made my way back to Lee and Jade with slumped shoulders.

Lee looked at me. "Do you think we will ever find Mother and Father?"

I remembered Mother's kiss on our foreheads before we left. I touched my finger to where Mother had kissed Lee.

"I do," I said. "I really do think we will find them."

I handed him and Jade a few items of clothes from our basket. We rolled up pants to use as pillows and wrapped shirts over us as blankets.

Lee scooted up to me, snuggling his body against mine.

"You know," he said. "This is exactly how cowboys sleep—under the stars. Lily, I think you're tougher than any outlaws in any of the stories I've read."

I laid down next him. Jade rested next to me.

"I don't know about outlaws, but I certainly *smell* like a cowboy right now," I said.

Lee managed to laugh. "We stink more than wild horses."

After a few minutes, Lee grew quiet and his breathing deepened.

As he and Jade drifted to sleep, I wondered where my parents were. Did they escape Chinatown? Were they mistaken for looters and shot by the soldiers? Why were they not here waiting for us at the Ferry Building?

I hardly slept at all. The ground was cold and hard. Strangers walked all around us all night. Noises from people crying or talking also kept me up. Jade slept close to me and Lee. I saw her take her silver comb out of her hair and hold it in her hands. The sharp teeth of the comb pointed outward. I finally dozed off just to be awakened by a man kneeling next to us.

He was going through our basket.

CHAPTER **EIGHT**

Jade sat up and pointed the comb at his neck. "Get away from us," she said in Mandarin. Her hair spilled around her face, and her voice was a growl. She held her body at a sharp angle, ready to strike.

The man dropped my book and held up his hands. He backed away and fled.

"Jade," Lee said, his eyes wide open. "You're my number-one outlaw!"

Jade glared after the man. "No one will bother us anymore," she said as she tucked her comb back in her hair. "I will protect us."

The crowd of people were starting to wake. With no food left, Lee, Jade, and I went without breakfast. Though we were hungry, the new day brought hope. We gathered up our things and walked around the Ferry Building again.

After a few minutes, I saw a familiar head of hair. White streaks in a long black braid. The man turned his head, and I recognized my friend.

"Mr. Quan!" I shouted.

Mr. Quan turned. "Lily! Lee! Jade! I found you!" He rushed over to us, grinning. "I heard from others about a young Chinese girl, standing up to a bunch of mean people!" he said. "I wondered if this brave girl was you, Lily."

I held my hands to my cheeks. I was blushing, but this time, I didn't duck my head. "It was me," I said. "You should have seen Lee and Jade too. We almost got trampled by a runaway steer, and we lost our laundry basket, but Lee found it. Jade also scared away a person who was trying to steal from us."

Mr. Quan smiled. "You all run wild, like the horses," he said. "No one had better get in your way."

I wrapped my arms around my friend. "I am so happy to see you."

He hugged me back. "Your parents and June are already in Oakland. They are safe."

Lee jumped up and down. "You saw them! How did they make it out?"

"Your father was able to get a ride for your mother and the baby," Mr. Quan said. "I saw them yesterday, right here at this park!"

Jade reached out to Lee and me. "Your parents are so very close," she said.

Mr. Quan hung his head. "I told your father to take your mother and sister to Oakland on the first ferry they could get. I felt so terrible that I was separated from you all and promised to stay here until I found you."

"I'm glad they are safe, but I wish we hadn't missed them," I said. I was disappointed to know I had been so close to being reunited with my parents yesterday.

"Good news!" Mr. Quan said. "Your mother's leg isn't broken after all. There was a doctor at the Ferry Building who looked at it. It is badly sprained, but she can walk. It was still best to get her out of the city as soon as they could so she can rest."

"I understand," Lee said, sounding like a grown-up. "Mother needed to get help."

I looked out at the bay. Just across the water, my parents were waiting for me. Oakland looked more promising than San Francisco right now. I tried to imagine them on the other side.

There were still thousands of people waiting

to leave San Francisco. In the distance, the city still burned. Somewhere in the chaos was Chinatown. From what I was hearing, I knew there would not be much left.

Jade, who had been quiet this entire time, stood up. "I'm ready to leave this place," she said. "Chinatown is no longer my home. I will start over."

Lee stood next to her. "We are ready to go too," he said.

I looked across the water. "Let's go find our parents."

CHAPTER NINE

Ferry Building, San Francisco
April 19, 1906
Thursday morning, 6:00 a.m.

As the sun moved higher in the sky, the crowd of people surrounding the wharf also grew bigger.

"How are we going to get on a boat?" I said. "Everyone wants to do the same thing."

Mr. Quan tapped his finger on his chin. "It will be difficult," he said. "I overheard people offer money or help loading cargo. I know you all can't lift heavy things, but maybe if I offer our labor they can take all of us."

Jade looked doubtful. "Why would they take us in Oakland? No one in San Francisco wants us here."

I caught her eyes. "I want you here."

Jade looked at me. "Thank you," she said.

Mr. Quan slapped his knee. "We are Chinese. We are strong people. We have made it this far and will continue to go farther. We will get to Oakland."

He turned to me and Lee. "Your father is probably finding us work there right now. I'm sure your mother is resting at your cousin's home this very moment. They are probably preparing for you both to arrive."

I could picture Mother. She would be sitting in a chair, with June in her lap. June would be sucking on her fingers and drooling from her brand-new teeth. I couldn't wait to see my baby sister again.

We packed up our meager belongings. I placed my book in the basket. It would be good to get to Oakland and have a better meal. I wanted to take a bath, then sit next to my parents and read my new book.

I understood what Dorothy meant when she said there was no place like home. It was sad to think our apartment was probably ruined by now—either by fire or by people tearing it down to create a firebreak. But I knew that it didn't matter where we lived. I just wanted us all to be together again. That would be home enough for me.

We made our way across the park. Several boats and ferries lined the shore of the harbor. There were many more people than there was room on the boats.

A crowd swelled around the shore. People waved money in the air. Some held out sparkling jewelry. Mothers held their children up. "Save my baby!" they cried.

"Take us, please!" someone else yelled.

"We need to get out of here!"

"Help us!"

Somehow Mr. Quan led our group through the crowd to the front of the line. He waved to a man on the boat.

"Hello!" Mr. Quan said in English. "We would like to help load cargo if the captain could take us all across to Oakland."

The man looked at us. "What do they have to offer?"

Jade took a silver comb out of her hair. She handed it to the man. "For you," she said in English. "For freedom."

The captain turned the comb over with his fingers. He seemed satisfied. "It's a pretty thing, isn't it?"

He looked at my brother and me. "Well?" he said, pointing at us. "What do you both have to offer? Any more Chinese trinkets?"

Lee looked at me. I looked at Lee. We both

knew we didn't have much. All we had was our clothes we'd packed in the laundry basket. Our food was gone, and the basket was worth practically nothing.

Then I saw my copy of *The Wonderful Wizard of Oz*. I swallowed. With dirty fingers, I picked up the book. It had only been mine for two days, but it felt like a lifetime. I had read to Lee from it on my birthday. I had used it to dig out from under the table. The book had given me strength during my journey. I'd remembered each character as I followed my own yellow brick road.

I felt sad knowing I was about to give up my most valuable possession. But being with my family again would be even better. That was worth more than all the stories in the world.

"I will give you this book," I told the captain. "It's my favorite story."

The captain frowned. He lifted up his hand and

swatted the book out of my grip. "What am I going to do with an old book?" he asked.

My book tumbled into the crowd. "No!" I yelled.

My shout caused a stir in the crowd. Suddenly, they all began to push.

"Get out of my way!" people shouted.

In one huge surge, hundreds of people swarmed the deck. I felt hands on my back and elbows in my sides.

I reached for Lee's hand, but it was too late.

My brother was swallowed up in the crowd.

CHAPTER **TEN**

San Francisco Bay
April 19, 1906
Thursday morning, 8:00 a.m.

"Lee!" I yelled. "Lee, where are you?"

My voice was lost in the masses. There was screaming and pushing all around me. I found myself being swept up into the swarm of people. Suddenly I found myself pushed right onto the boat. Into a sea of strangers.

"Lee!" I said again. "Jade! Mr. Quan! Where are you?"

I tried to push my way off the boat, but the force of people trying to get on wouldn't let me.

"Keep going!" someone shouted.

"You're going the wrong way!"

"Hurry up!" yelled another.

There was a loud boom. The captain slammed the door to the boat shut. "That's it!" he said. "No more passengers. All of you already on? You're lucky. You got yourself a free ride. I just want to be done with you all." He pointed to the crowd on the land. "The rest of you can wait for the next ship."

Those left on the pier shouted in anger. "Take us!" they cried.

"Don't leave me behind!"

The captain took off his cap and waved it to the crowd. "We are coming right back!" he said. "Hold on to your britches, ships are coming to get you all day long." He shook his head. "No order here," he muttered. "No order at all."

As the boat began to pull away, I looked helplessly into the crowd still on land.

The captain had said that those on the boat were

some of the fortunate ones. I didn't feel so lucky. This was not how I imagined escaping San Francisco. This was not how I was supposed to leave Chinatown. My hands were empty. I had nothing. I had left Lee behind on his own. He was so small. How would he find his way? I had escaped, but I had let my family down. I had lost Lee.

"Oh no, no, no, no, no," I said. "No, no, no, no, no."

I was alone, and I was terrified. I leaned over the edge of the ship and spotted a familiar head back on the pier. "Mr. Quan!" I yelled. I waved my arms.

He saw me and waved back. Mr. Quan was shouting something to me. Above the sounds of the ocean spray and noise of the ferry departing, I struggled to hear his words.

"Be brave!" he seemed to say. "Be brave, Lily!"

I wasn't sure if I was imagining his words,

or if I was telling them to myself. I wanted to be adventurous like Dorothy. Brave like the Cowardly Lion. Have a heart like the Tin Woodman. Be smart like the Scarecrow. But I was none of these things. I wanted to go back to before the earthquake, when I would wake up next to Lee on our living room floor. I wanted to duck under the blankets and never come out again.

As the ferry pulled away from the harbor, I held on to the ship rail to keep from falling over. I was so tired. For the first time in days, I was also alone.

I had failed to do the one thing I'd promised my parents—to keep Lee safe.

Lake Merritt Harbor, Oakland
April 19, 1906
Thursday morning, 10:00 a.m.

The ferry ride to Oakland felt like an eternity. If I did find my mother and father, what would

I say? How could I tell them that I'd lost Lee at the very last minute?

I held on to the railing and watched San Francisco grow smaller. It was billowing with smoke and flames. I closed my eyes. I imagined my home, gone. The grocery store, gone. My book, gone. And now Lee was gone.

"Lily, Lily!" someone shouted, shaking me from my thoughts.

Fingers dug into my arm. Lee! I blinked, like I was slowly coming out from a dream. There was a roaring in my ears. It took a moment for me to realize that the screams were coming from my own mouth.

"Yippee!" I whooped.

I was so happy, I didn't care if the entire ferry heard me. I hoped my parents could hear me all the way in Oakland and that Jade and Mr. Quan could hear me in San Francisco.

I wrapped my arms around my brother. "You're here!" I exclaimed. "You are the smelliest cowboy to ever walk the earth, and I am so happy to see you."

"Hey!" Lee said. He crossed his arms and smiled. "I thought *you* were the smelliest cowboy."

I smiled back. "We can both be the smelliest."

Lee laughed. "Mother will love that."

I laughed too. "You bet she will."

I didn't let go of Lee's hand for the rest of the boat ride. When the ferry docked, Lee and I followed a group of Chinese people off the boat. Where Chinese people gathered, I knew I would find my parents. I touched my forehead. Mother's kiss had kept us safe.

The Oakland port was huge. Lee and I walked around together. We stood near where the Chinese people had gathered, but we didn't see Mother or Father—or anyone we knew.

We went back closer to the ferry. No luck there. I couldn't believe this. After all this traveling, we still couldn't find our parents. Lee and I went back to where most of the Chinese people were.

Lee and I sat down on the edge of the crowd.

"Now what?" Lee asked.

"I guess we wait," I said. "Mr. Quan should get on another boat. Hopefully we will find him."

"Did you ever see Jade?" Lee asked.

I thought of the comb Jade gave away. "No," I said. "I didn't."

Just then, we heard a familiar cry. It was fussy and bossy, like a baby whose teeth were coming in. Slowly, Lee and I stood up. We followed the baby's cries through the crowd. She sounded like our sister, June. The screams were like a trail of breadcrumbs leading us out of the forest.

The crowd parted, and I saw a man bouncing a baby on his hip. The man was facing the other way, but I would recognize those chubby baby cheeks anywhere. Behind him, a woman rested on a crate, holding a piece of bread.

"June!" Lee yelled.

"Father, Mother!" I shouted.

Lee and I broke into a run.

Mother stood up and dropped her piece of bread. Father turned around. Baby June stopped crying.

Lee and I flung ourselves into the arms of our parents. Father wrapped his warm arms around me. Mother hugged Lee close. Baby June pulled our hair.

We were reunited at last.

We had made it home. There was no place like it.

A NOTE FROM THE AUTHOR

On Wednesday, April 18, 1906, 5:12 a.m.,
a devastating earthquake hit San Francisco. Although
the earthquake and aftershocks were powerful, they did
not cause serious damage to the structures in Chinatown.
However, widespread fires broke out over other areas
of the city and many water lines were down. In order
to save San Francisco, the firefighters chose to create a
firebreak, or a clear area, where Chinatown was. They
used explosives to blow up the existing buildings in
Chinatown and sacrificed the homes and businesses of
the people who lived there.

Unfortunately, instead of stopping the fire, the
dynamite caused new fires. By the next day, all of
Chinatown was reduced to ashes. The fire burned for
four days.

At the time of the 1906 earthquake, about 400,000
people lived in San Francisco. City officials set the
number of those who died in the earthquake and fires at
300. In this death count, they did not include any of the
14,000 or so Chinese people who lived in Chinatown.

About 25,000 buildings were destroyed in the fires.

No one knows how many Chinese immigrants died in the earthquake and fire.

Today, researchers estimate that close to 3,000 people lost their lives. The researchers believe that city officials at the time reported a lower number of fatalities so investors would not be scared away from rebuilding San Francisco.

During this time, hatred and racism against Chinese immigrants was very high. Like other immigrants at the time, many Chinese people came to the United States for better opportunities. They were paid lower wages than their white working counterparts, and were then blamed for driving down pay and taking away jobs.

The Chinese Exclusion Act was a law put into place in 1882 to not allow any more immigrants from China. It was the first time the United States restricted immigration based on race. Many of the men who came to the United States to work would not be able to bring their families over. Because of this law, there were few Chinese women and girls who could come to America.

A Chinese man looked out over the ruins of Chinatown following the 1906 earthquake.

Chinatown was in a good location in San Francisco and the land was very valuable. After the fire, San Francisco officials took the destruction of Chinatown as an opportunity to relocate the Chinese population to a less desirable area. The Chinatown residents did not want to give up their home. The empress of China was unhappy with the plan to move Chinatown. She had intended to rebuild the Chinese Consulate in the heart of Chinatown. Fearing the city would lose tax dollars and valuable trade with China, the officials dropped their plans.

When the time came to rebuild Chinatown, a businessman named Look Tin Eli convinced residents to make the new Chinatown a tourist attraction. They hired American architects to redesign the buildings with pagodas and colorful designs. They had dragons on top and curved rooftops, just as the Americans imagined China looked like.

I use the term "Americans" in reference to white Americans during this time. Even though Lily and her family were born in the United States, many white people did not consider them Americans. I don't think

Lily's family considered themselves American either. They weren't allowed to attend school with white children, they had to live in a certain area, and the Chinese Exclusion Act wasn't repealed until 1943.

For this book, I was inspired by the account of Lily Sung, a seven-year-old girl who survived the 1906 earthquake in San Francisco. Like the Lily I wrote about, Lily Sung also heard cats screeching the night before the devastating earthquake. She traveled in a group with her siblings and a woman with bound feet to be reunited with her family. Lily Sung's birth certificate and family documents were destroyed in the Chinatown fires. In 1922, she lost her American citizenship because of the Chinese Exclusion Act. Lily Sung was very brave. I hope there is some of her blossoming in the fictionalized Lily I wrote about.

I lived in San Francisco when I was a kid. I was actually in the Loma Prieta earthquake on October 17, 1989 that killed 63 people. Even though I am Chinese American, lived in San Francisco, and often went to Chinatown, I didn't learn about the racism against Chinese immigrants in school. I wasn't aware of the

The Loma Prieta earthquake caused severe damage to buildings throughout Oakland and San Francisco.

segregated schools or living areas. I didn't know the extent of the Chinese Exclusion Act until I began research for this book.

Chinese American experiences and stories are not widely known. Writing Lily's story has given me chance to examine a piece of history that has long gone unnoticed. I hope you've also been able to find inspiration in Lily's journey and her chance to be seen.

GLOSSARY

aftershock (AF-tur-shahk)—a small earthquake that comes after a larger one

bao (BOW)—a bread-like dough usually filled and steamed in Chinese cuisine for dumplings and buns

bubonic plague (boo-BON-ik PLAYG)—a disease spread by rats that causes fever, weakness, and swollen lymph nodes

cable car (KAY-buhl kahr)—vehicle used for public transportation that moves on a suspended cable

Chinatown (CHYE-nuh-toun)—an area outside of Mainland China where many Chinese people live

debris (duh-BREE)—pieces of broken objects

eternity (i-TUR-nih-tee)—a seemingly endless amount of time

ferry (FEH-ree)—a large ship or boat used to transport passengers or goods

firebreak (FIRE-brayk)—an area of open or clear land used to stop the spreading of a fire

immigrant (IM-ih-gruhnt)—a person who comes to live permanently in a country they weren't born in

looter (LOOT-er)—a person who steals during a crisis, like a war or natural disaster

Mandarin (MAN-duh-rin)—one of the major languages in China

outlaw (OUT-law)—someone who has broken the law

Penny Dreadful (PEN-ee DRED-fuhl)—affordable, popular books published in the nineteenth century

Presbyterian (press-bih-TAIR-ee-uhn)—a Protestant Christian church

restriction (ree-STRIK-shuhn)—a limit on the use of a property or area

steeple (STEE-puhl)—a high tower on a church, often with a spire on top

steer (STEER)—a young male bull, usually raised for beef

tremor (TREM-ur)—a small earthquake, or a shaking movement

vermin (VUR-min)—wild animals that carry disease

MAKING CONNECTIONS

1. Lily lost her home to the fires in Chinatown. How do you think she will rebuild her new life? How would you do the same if you were in her situation?

2. How did the characters from Lily's favorite book, *The Wonderful Wizard of Oz*, help her on her journey? How did this book give her hope?

3. Do you see similarities between the prejudice the Chinese immigrants experienced in 1906 and the prejudice some people experience today? Explain.

ABOUT THE AUTHOR

Veeda Bybee grew up collecting passport stamps and
dreaming of castles in far-off places. A daughter of
Asian immigrants, she has been writing and drawing
pictures since she was seven years old. She is a former
journalist and has an MFA in Creative Writing from
Vermont College of Fine Arts. She lives in Nevada with
her family, where she reads, writes, and bakes.